D0121469

The new girl gives Nicole a little concert fever.

PUFFIN BOOKS

The English Roses

The New Girl

PUFFIN BOOKS

Published by the Penguin Group
Penguin Books Ltd, 80 Strand, London WC2R 0RL, England
Penguin Group (USA) Inc., 375 Hudson Street, New York, New York 10014, USA
Penguin Group (Canada), 90 Eglinton Avenue East, Suite 700, Toronto, Ontario, Canada M4P 2Y3
(a division of Pearson Penguin Canada Inc.)
Penguin Ireland, 25 St Stephen's Green, Dublin 2, Ireland (a division of Penguin Books Ltd)
Penguin Group (Australia), 250 Camberwell Road, Camberwell, Victoria 3124, Australia
(a division of Pearson Australia Group Pty Ltd)
Penguin Books India Pvt Ltd, 11 Community Centre, Panchsheel Park, New Delhi – 110 017, India
Penguin Group (NZ), 67 Apollo Drive, Mairangi Bay, Auckland 1310, New Zealand
(a division of Pearson New Zealand Ltd)
Penguin Books (South Africa) (Pty) Ltd, 24 Sturdee Avenue, Rosebank, Johannesburg 2196, South Africa

Penguin Books Ltd, Registered Offices: 80 Strand, London WC2R 0RL, England

puffinbooks.com

First published in the USA in 2007
Designed by Toshiya Masuda and produced by Callaway Arts & Entertainment
First published in Great Britain in Puffin Books 2008
1

Copyright © Madonna, 2007
All rights reserved

The moral right of the author and illustrator has been asserted

Fluffernutter is a registered trademark of Durkee-Mower, Inc. and is used by permission.
All rights reserved

Made and printed in Italy

British Library Cataloguing in Publication Data
A CIP catalogue record for this book is available from the British Library

ISBN: 978-0-141-38379-8

All of Madonna's proceeds from this book will be donated to
Raising Malawi (www.raisingmalawi.org), an orphan-care initiative.

The English Roses

by MADONNA

With Amy Cloud

The New Girl

PUFFIN

illustrated by jeffrey fulvimari

Book 3

Contents

CHAPTER I

Guess Who's Coming to London?

TOWER BRIDGE

If you still have not heard of the English Roses, then I am very afraid, my dear, that your headphones have been plugging your ears for a teensy bit too long. Either that or you're spending too much time poring over fashion mags. Or perhaps you're spending all your time at the cinema? At any rate, you'd best listen up, because these English Roses are too cool for school (well, they're actually very good students, but you get the idea).

The English Roses are five girls named Nicole, Amy, Charlotte, Grace and Binah. They are best friends and they do everything – and I do mean everything – together: birthday bashes, shopping extravaganzas, horror movie nights, fancy-dress parties, study groups and dance classes. There are more, but I can't name them all; it's not like I have all day just to tell you about them!

Anyway, these five girls love each other dearly, though each one is as different as can be. And, you know, as with any group of friends, they're bound to argue now and then. In fact, I know of one time in particular when they did just that. It all start-

ed on a pleasant autumn day, the kind of day so deliciously cool that you are able to wear your favourite scarf and jumper for the first time that season. It was on such a seemingly perfect day that all the trouble began.

* * *

'Ni-co-ole,' sang Grace, squeezing her best friend's arm. 'Why are you being so qu-i-et, Miss Moody?'

Nicole shook her head, as if awakening from a dream. She had been thinking about school – in particular, about her year-eight teacher, Mrs Moss, who had scolded her earlier for writing song lyrics during maths instead of learning how to add fractions. It's just that adding fractions was so utterly boring, how could Mrs Moss possibly expect her to pay attention? Besides, wasn't writing lyrics for the next hit single more important than adding silly numbers? Before she could respond, her other best friend, Amy, piped up.

'Don't be sad, Nikki,' soothed Amy, twirling her hair thoughtfully. 'Just think about something that's too good to be true. Like . . . a room filled with every kind of designer handbag.'

The girls shrieked with excitement as they turned down Nicole's street, Primrose Lane.

Nicole smiled, then rolled her eyes. She loved Amy dearly, but she was always gushing about clothes and accessories. Nicole liked clothes all right, but how many times could you scream over a handbag?

As I mentioned, it was a nearly perfect autumn afternoon in London – and you know how rare those are, don't you? The sky seemed a shade or two bluer than usual, and soft, puffy clouds danced their way across the horizon. There was a wonderful crispness in the air as the English Roses – Nicole, Grace, Amy, Charlotte and Binah – walked to

Nicole's house for milkshakes after a quite spectacular day at school. Well, it had been spectacular for everyone except Nicole: Grace had scored five points playing football during PE; Charlotte had received a wink and smile from her biggest crush, William Worthington, during their Spanish lesson; Amy's drawing had been picked to be in the autumn art show; and Binah had got an A on her history paper.

'MU-UM, we're hooo-oome!!!' Nicole threw open the front door and, one by one, her best friends walked in after her, politely slipping off their shoes and hanging their jackets in the closet.

'Hello, girls,' Nicole's mother called from the kitchen. 'I'm making some milkshakes – extra thick, just the way you like them!'

'Good afternoon, Mrs Rissman,' Charlotte said primly, gingerly placing her handbag on the counter. Her smile revealed a row of perfectly straight white teeth. 'It's so nice to see you, as always!'

Charlotte had the best manners of all the girls.

Her parents were very wealthy, and she had actually been sent to charm school as a child. The English Roses were forever teasing her about it.

'And how are the English Roses this afternoon?' Mrs Rissman asked, kissing Nicole on the top of her messy blonde head. 'You're all looking exceptionally lovely, I must say.'

The girls giggled.

'We're fine,' Nicole replied briskly. 'I'm going to check my email quickly, okay?' she shouted, flying up the stairs to her bedroom.

'What's wrong with Nicole today?' Mrs Rissman asked, filling four tall glasses with frothy milkshakes, and a fifth (for Nicole, who didn't eat dairy because it upset her tummy) with a strawberry smoothie.

'Oh, you know Nicole,' Grace responded, shaking her crazy pigtails and slurping her shake. 'She's just in one of her moods. I think Mrs Moss was picking on her.'

'I hope she's okay,' said Binah softly. 'I know it can be a bummer when Mrs Moss scolds you in front of the whole class.'

'Well, we all know Nicole and her moods,' Mrs Rissman responded with a smile. 'Sometimes I think I should have named her Miss Moody!'

The girls giggled again as they sipped their shakes. Mrs Rissman was just the sort of mother everyone wanted. She was funny (really funny – not stuffy grown-up funny) and kind and had velvety-brown eyes that crinkled in the corners when she smiled. You could hear her big, hearty laugh from across the street, and she always gave the best advice. She also made the best milkshakes, which is why the girls loved going to Nicole's house after school.

Nicole threw her backpack on her bedroom floor, which was littered with sweet wrappers and pyjamas and CDs. 'I'll clean it up later,' she thought, switching on her computer. She could hear her friends giggling downstairs, and a bit of guilt pricked at her heart. She knew she should be down there with them, but sometimes a girl just needed a moment alone.

'You've got mail!' the computer barked, and Nicole's heart soared. She loved hearing that sound! Adjusting her glasses, she read a message eagerly:

From: Leslie Loehmann

Subject: THE BIGGEST NEWS!!!

Date: Tuesday, September 14 2:50 AM EST

To: Nicole Rissman

NIKKI!

How are you?

It's super-duper late here in New York, but I couldn't sleep, and just had to write you. I have the most superb, totally fantastic news: my dad is filming a new movie and shooting part of it in London. Which means I AM MOVING TO LONDON FOR THREE WHOLE MONTHS! (Sorry to scream, but I'm so excited.) You and I will be neighbors!!

I'll miss New York tons, I'm sure, but you know how

I love to travel, and I can't wait to see what London is all about! Bangers and mash, Big Ben, and cute British boys . . . sounds like my cup of tea! Can you believe we'll be living in the same city? It will be just like last summer in the Hamptons!

OK, gotta go to bed now.

By the way, have you finished writing your song? I'm dying to hear it.

Call me!!!

<3 <3 <3 always,
Les

Nicole danced and pranced around the room, giddy with excitement. She had met Leslie last summer when Nicole's father, a diplomat, brought the family along to New York City on a business trip for three months. Nicole had spent a few weeks in the Hamptons – a posh community located on the eastern tip of Long Island – and she had met Leslie on the beach. Both girls were listening to their iPods instead of splashing in the water and, as it turned out, Leslie was one of the few girls she met in East Hampton who loved music and writing as much as she did. They became fast friends and spent days lounging at the beach, listening to tunes, gossiping about the lifeguards, painting their toenails and riding the waves on body boards. Leslie was glamorous and smart and very sophisticated.

She was filled with fun stories about famous people her dad knew and life in New York. Nicole missed her a lot.

'This is so cool!' Nicole squealed out loud. She felt dizzy from the exhilaration of it all: Leslie's father was directing a movie, Leslie was asking about her song, but most exciting of all: LESLIE WAS COMING TO LONDON.

Nicole raced downstairs to tell her friends all about the big news. This day was turning out to be quite spectacular, even for Nicole. Leslie might just become the sixth English Rose!

CHAPTER 2

The Funky Five

announcing the
WE'VE
GOT
TALENT
CONTEST !!

Two weeks later, the English Roses were
at Grace's house having one of their regu-
lar after–school hangout sessions. Grace
was lounging on her bed; Amy, Charlotte
and Binah were sprawled on the floor;
and Nicole was slouched on Grace's beanbag chair.
They were all giggling over the fact that Amy's

crush, Ryan Hudson, had winked at her during science. 'It was while we were dissecting frogs! I mean, he had a piece of frog intestine in his hand! Who does that?' she snorted.

'Maybe,' Binah offered, 'he has a special love for frogs, and that made him think of you. Or maybe frog dissection is his hidden talent, and –'

Suddenly, Grace looked up and exclaimed, 'Wait a minute! Speaking of talent, isn't the We've Got Talent Competition coming up? We have to figure out what we're doing, pronto!'

Their school's We've Got Talent Competition was the most highly anticipated event of the year. The winning performers received a gift certificate to Harrods, the coolest department store in London, and a day of fun activities with Miss Fluffernutter,

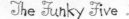

the English Roses' beloved year-seven teacher, who was in charge of the competition. The English Roses always did something together, of course!

'Well, we could do a skit, like we did last year,' Charlotte suggested.

'Nah, we have to do something new, and something really fab!' Amy insisted, waving her hands about dramatically. 'Something that will blow everyone away.'

'I know,' Grace suggested, 'why don't we do a really sensational dance? Since my mom's a dance teacher, I could ask her to help me choreograph it.'

All the girls agreed that this was a brill idea, except for Nicole.

'The skit may be fun too,' she said in a hopeful voice. The truth was that deep down inside she

i ♡ dancing

hated precise dance routines. She preferred to move as she liked, as the music made her feel.

'Nah, Amy's right, we did a skit last year,' Binah said. 'A dance would be super-cool. We could call ourselves . . . the Funky Five!'

The other girls squealed with excitement.

Nicole felt she couldn't say no when her friends

seemed to have their hearts set on doing the dance. 'Okay,' she smiled, 'I'm game!'

* * *

An hour later, Grace had steered the group into her family's basement, where they began working out the first steps of their routine.

'And next, we're going to do a hip swivel, like this,' Grace said, demonstrating a small shake of her hips. 'And then slide into splits, one by one.'

'But I can't do the splits,' said Charlotte.

'And I can't shake my hips,' Nicole added.

'Yes you can!' Amy told her. 'You're one of the best dancers in our school!'

What? You don't believe Amy? Well, let me tell just how good a dancer Nicole really was: she was

known throughout school as the Dancing Machine. At parties, crowds formed around her as she demonstrated her cooler-than-you moves. Now, can we get back to the rest of the story?

'Well, anyway, I can teach you. In fact, let's spend all day Saturday learning the splits and shaking our hips.' Grace giggled at her own rhyme. 'It's really easy once you practise,' she told them, sliding down into a perfect split. 'Ta-da!'

Nicole racked her brain for excuses to get out of practice. 'Actually, oh no! I have plans,' she said, contorting her face into a sour expression. 'I'm . . . uh . . . looking after our neighbour's . . . pet . . . pig.' As soon as the words escaped her lips, she felt her face flushing! She was always the worst at coming up with believable excuses.

'The Dolmeyers have a pet pig?' Amy asked, wrinkling her nose. 'Is that even legal?'

'Uh ... well, no ... actually, I just made that up,' Nicole admitted guiltily. 'I really have to work on my song. I'm almost finished,' she added.

'Cool,' said Charlotte. 'Will you sing it for us, Nicole? Please?'

'Sorry, but not yet,' Nicole said nervously. 'I want to make sure it's perfect before anyone hears it.'

'Well, um, before you do that, I need help,' Grace said wearily, still in the splits position. 'I can't get up!'

The other girls giggled as they pulled Grace to her feet.

'Just so you all know, I'll be toast in maths tomorrow,' Charlotte said, flicking her shiny black hair behind her shoulders. 'Patrick the Pest strikes again! He thought it would be humorous to blow his slimy bogeys all over my homework this afternoon.' Charlotte's little brother was always torturing her in some way.

Amy snorted. 'That's sort of funny.'

'It is NOT funny,' Charlotte fumed. 'It's just more evidence that I'm the unfortunate sibling of a troll-faced monster!'

After-school snack.

'All right, all right, calm down,' interrupted Grace. 'So, are you ladies going to be able to practise some more after school tomorrow? We only have a week left.'

All the girls agreed, except for Nicole. She started gnawing on her nails, a bad habit she was forever trying to break.

'Um, well, actually,' she began, 'I forgot that Leslie arrived in town yesterday, and I promised to help her unpack tomorrow, so . . .'

'That's okay, Nicole,' Binah said, doing a little tap dance on the spot. 'We can all practise another day. Right, girls?'

'I guess so,' Grace muttered. 'But we don't have much time. If we want to win this thing, and I think we do –' she narrowed her eyes and looked around – 'we have to practise our steps as much as possible.'

Grace was the sporty one of the group, and had a huge competitive streak.

'So, when are we going to get to meet Leslie?' asked Amy, eager to change the subject.

'Soon!' Nicole said. 'I just know you guys are going to love her. She's just so cool and sophisticated, but, like, super-smart and just . . . like, you want to be her, to have her life, kind of.'

The other girls looked at each other. Ever since she heard Leslie was moving to London, Nicole wouldn't stop gushing about how great Leslie was,

how totally brill, how smart and gorgeous and talented. Truthfully, they were getting a bit tired of always
hearing about her.

'Well, I gotta go now,' Nicole said, hugging her
four best friends and slinging her backpack across her
shoulder. 'See you in Mrs Moss's class tomorrow.'

CHAPTER 3

New York State of Mind

'Okay, tell me the truth, Nikki,' Leslie giggled, holding up a blindingly bright neon-pink leopard-print top. 'This won't fly in London, right?'

Nicole looked up from her spot on the floor, where she was lazily sorting through boxes of Leslie's clothing. 'Well,' she began, 'truthfully, it's a little . . . much for our school.'

'So, you're saying that no British girl would be caught dead in this,' she said, tossing the unfortunate top into a bin clearly marked THROW AWAY. 'I have to tell you, I'm soooo nervous about my first day tomorrow.'

'Don't be! I just know everyone will think you're the coolest thing London's seen in years!' Nicole reassured her. 'Especially the English Roses.'

'I certainly hope so.' Leslie sighed dramatically, flopping down on the bed. 'I'm kind of scared they won't like me, or that they'll think I'm some American idiot.'

'There's no way they could ever think that,' Nicole insisted. 'You're fabulous. They are going to love you to death!'

'We'll see,' Leslie said, not sounding convinced. 'I'm tired of unpacking. I obviously need new clothes if I'm gonna fit in here – let's go shopping!'

Giggling, the two girls ran downstairs to ask for a lift to the high street. Nicole couldn't wait to show Leslie the most bangin' shops in London.

*   *   *

Her arms filled with bursting shopping bags, Leslie kissed Nicole on the cheek as they left her

favourite store. 'Thanks so much for going shopping with me, Nikki. You're the best friend ever!'

'I know,' Nicole said with a smile. 'But, just so you know, if you ever again make me sit there while you try on every single piece of clothing in the entire store, I might have to kill you!'

'I'm sorry! I guess I'm just picky,' Leslie said, giggling. 'Can I make it up to you with a smoothie?'

'That could work.' Nicole grinned.

The friends popped into the best ice-cream parlour in town, Oddono's, and sauntered up to the counter. Leslie ordered a strawberry gelato, and Nicole had just ordered a berrylicious smoothie when she felt a tap on her shoulder. She whirled round to find Amy standing behind her, a befuddled expression on her face.

'Hey, Nicole!' exclaimed Amy. 'What's up? I thought you had to help your friend unpack today.'

'W-well, we were, sorta,' stammered Nicole, 'but then Leslie needed new clothes, and . . . you know.' She looked beyond Amy to see the three other Roses at their usual corner table, sharing hot-fudge sundaes.

'Well, don't just stand there, silly,' Amy said. 'Why don't you come and join us!'

Nicole and Leslie sat down with the other girls. 'This is Leslie Loehmann. Leslie, these are the English Roses: Amy, Grace, Binah and Charlotte.'

The English Roses said hello, then paused as they took in the full picture that was Leslie Loehmann. She was tall – it seemed like almost a foot taller than the rest of them — with honey-coloured hair that ran in soft waves down her back. She was wearing tight blue jeans perfectly tucked into black boots, a grey newsboy cap and a fitted maroon vest over a white T-shirt. Her big blue eyes were framed

by the thickest, curliest lashes they had ever seen. The English Roses were, to be sure, fairly stylish girls, but Leslie put them all to shame. She looked like she was at least fifteen.

'Sooooo glad to finally meet you British dolls!' Leslie babbled.

'It's nice to meet you too, Leslie,' Charlotte responded. 'What a cool hat!'

'Oh, this old thing? You really like it?' Leslie gushed. 'It's really no big deal! Just something my father picked up on his trip to Paris last year.'

The girls were impressed that anyone's father could pick out something so fashionable.

'Oh, and your necklace is just ADORABLE!' Leslie shrieked, fingering Binah's golden locket. 'My housekeeper's daughter has one exactly like it.'

Now, if you're thinking, no, she did not just say that to Binah – the same Binah whose father had to work two jobs to make ends meet; the same Binah who was already self-conscious that she did not have as much money as the rest of the English Roses – let me assure you, she certainly did! But it's not entirely her fault, for she had no idea about Binah's home life. Would you have if I hadn't told you?

The English Roses just looked at each other warily. Binah flushed a deep crimson. What could one say to something like that?

Leslie eyed the rest of the girls. 'So,' she remarked, 'it looks like you eat a lot more ice cream over here than we do in the States.'

There was an awkward silence. Finally Grace spoke up.

'Well, we weren't originally going to come here today. We would have been practising our talent-show dance,' she remarked icily, 'but Nicole had . . . other plans.'

'Talent show!' Leslie exclaimed. 'How utterly divine! Nikki, we should totally perform your amazing song!' She turned to the English Roses. 'Isn't Nikki's song just the most fabulous thing you've ever heard?'

The girls looked slightly hurt. 'We haven't heard it yet, actually,' Amy said.

Nicole nervously spoke up. 'Actually, Leslie, we – the English Roses – are doing a super-cool dance for the show. We're going to be called the Funky Five.'

Leslie looked baffled. 'A dance? But you hate

choreographed dance routines, Nikki,' she said.

The English Roses looked confused. 'You never told us that, Nicole,' Binah pointed out.

'Well, it's not – it's not exactly true,' Nicole replied quickly, slurping the rest of her smoothie. 'Listen, I have to be going now. My daddy's actually in town tonight so we're having a family dinner at home.' Nicole's dad was always travelling for work, and thus it was a special occasion when he could spend a few evenings with the family.

'It was absolutely fabulous meeting you ladies,' Leslie gushed. 'See you in school tomorrow.' She grabbed Nicole's hand and rushed out of the door.

The English Roses looked at each other.

'She was . . . weird,' said Grace. "British dolls'? That kind of makes me want to barf.'

'And what's with her outfit? She looked way too grown-up,' added Charlotte.

'And mean! What was that comment, we eat too much ice cream?' Amy demanded.

'Maybe she was just nervous,' Binah offered, 'and she didn't know what to say. It's not easy being the new kid in town.'

The girls thought about that. It was true she was new in town, and it was never easy moving to a new city – let alone a new country! They decided to give her the benefit of the doubt and be extra-friendly with her at school the next day.

Still, there was a tiny knot in the pit of each of their stomachs as they finished their sundaes.

CHAPTER 4

Dance Practice Disappointment

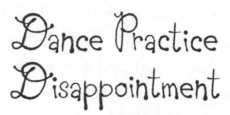

Every day at lunchtime, the English Roses sat together at the round table in the far-east corner of the cafeteria. It was a certainty in their school, as sure the sun rising in the east each morning and setting in the west each night. No matter which test had been failed, no matter which boy liked which girl or which girl liked which boy, Nicole, Charlotte, Amy, Binah and Grace filled the five chairs around that same table every single day at lunch.

Except that Thursday, when there were six chairs, not five. Nicole had asked if Leslie could join them. Remembering their earlier promise to be nice to Leslie, the English Roses didn't want to say no. But, truthfully, they weren't exactly tickled pink about the idea.

The girls were already giggling over their lunch

trays when Nicole and Leslie sat down. Once
again, Leslie looked years older than the other girls,
dressed to the nines in an outrageous red beret,
leggings, a grey-and-red striped tunic, and an
armful of bangles that jingled when she walked.

'It's so nice to see you again, Leslie,' Binah said
in a kind voice. 'How is your first day going?'

'Okay, I guess,' Leslie said, crunching on a car-
rot stick. 'I definitely miss being able to eat lunch in
Manhattan.'

'I miss the States sometimes too,' Grace offered.
'I'm from Atlanta originally.'

'Oh, yeah,' Leslie said, unenthused. 'I've never
really been . . . *there*.'

Grace looked slightly hurt. 'Well, I love London
now, and I'm sure you will too.'

'It's really awful that you couldn't be in Mrs
Moss's class with us,' Charlotte said, wrinkling her
nose. 'Mr Farburger is such a weirdo!'

'Oh, I know,' Leslie moaned, rolling her eyes.
'When he talks, bits of spit gather at the corners

of his mouth, and his face gets as red as a beet. It's sooo disgusting.'

'EWWW!' the rest of the girls giggled. Maybe Leslie isn't so bad after all, they thought.

'I just looooove your top, by the way,' Leslie said to Charlotte in a phoney-baloney voice. 'So very . . . *cute,* like a little girl. So innocent.'

'Um . . . thanks,' said Charlotte, who suddenly felt very much like the Mayor of Nerdville. She was wearing one of her favourites: a short-sleeved white blouse with pintucks and little embroidered roses. She had originally thought it was elegant, but Leslie was making her feel like a three-year-old!

'Yes, Charlotte has excellent taste,' Grace said, protectively taking her friend's arm.

Leslie looked sceptical. 'Maybe,' she said. 'But

you know who *really* has excellent taste – my father. He's shooting this amazingly touching film right now, here in London. I was soooo terribly moved by the script. He lets me read all his scripts, actually. His best script reader, that's what he calls me.'

Grace couldn't resist rolling her eyes, but Binah, ever the peacemaker, kicked her quickly under the table. 'OWWWWWW!' Grace howled.

Just then, Candy Darling came over to their lunch table. 'Howdy, English Roses. Are you fabulous ladies all ready for the talent show?'

'We're still practising,' Amy told her. 'How about you, Candy?'

'Bunny Love and I are doing another fantabulous tap dance. This one is bigger and better than ever. It's sure to be a bopping good time!'

Puh-leease don't tell me you don't know Bunny Love and her twin sister Candy Darling?! The two girls were excellent tap dancers and reigned supreme, along with Nicole, as being the dancing grande dames of the school. Sometimes the English Roses invited them to their sleepover parties.

'Candy, I'd like you to meet my friend Leslie,' Nicole said. 'She just moved here from New York.'

'Leslie Loehmann,' Leslie said professionally, sticking out her hand. 'Sooo lovely to meet you, Candy.'

'Nice to meet you too,' Candy replied. 'And welcome to this side of the pond! Well, I gotta go meet Miss Fluffernutter – she's tutoring me in maths.'

The girls said goodbye to Candy, and the conversation turned to the talent show.

'Practice after school today, girls,' Grace said loudly. 'I mean, we *have* to. No excuses this time.' She threw Nicole a sideways glance.

'What?' Nicole said, throwing up her hands. 'I didn't say I couldn't make this one!'

'Leslie, would you like to be in our talent show dance too?' asked Binah, realizing that Leslie probably felt a little left out. 'We could always use another pair of legs.'

'Oh, that's sooooo sweet of you to offer,' Leslie gushed. 'But, no, dancing's not really my thing. I'm more of a musician and muse, myself.'

The other girls, except for Nicole, breathed a silent sigh of relief. They didn't want this obnoxious new girl in their talent-show dance! They were convinced that, whatever she was, this impostor certainly was *not* an English Rose.

*   *   *

Later in the day, Nicole was walking back to class after a trip to the loo, when Leslie came flying at her, a whirlwind of excitement. She nearly ran Nicole down before crashing into a row of lockers.

'Leslie, are you okay?' Nicole asked, running over to her.

'Ow! Yeah, just clumsy as ever!' Leslie chuckled, rubbing her elbow. 'I was hoping I'd run into you! You won't believe this, but my daddy just called and told me he can get us into the sold-out Rachel Mint concert tonight. And –' she paused dramatically –

'there's a meet and greet before the show.'

'Rachel Mint?!' Nicole gasped. 'Really?' Her heart soared. Rachel Mint was one of her favourite singers!

'No joke,' Leslie said. 'The only thing is . . . we have to leave right after school. We need to get there super-early for the meet and greet.'

After school? Nicole vaguely remembered something she was supposed to do after school . . . dance practice! The English Roses were supposed to practise their routine for the talent show.

'Oh no,' she said, shaking her messy blonde ponytail in dismay. 'I told the Roses I'd be at Grace's for dance practice after school.'

Leslie shot her a sceptical look. 'Dance practice? This is Rachel Mint, Nikki. The hottest female singer/songwriter in, like, a million years. And we have a chance to *meet* her! Do you really want to miss that chance to practise a talent-show dance?'

Now that she thought about it, Nicole realized how silly it seemed to miss the concert for practice. After all, this was a once-in-a-lifetime opportunity. She was sure her friends would understand.

'I'm sure they'll understand,' Leslie said quickly, as if reading Nicole's mind.

'You're right,' she agreed, breaking into a huge grin. 'I have to ask my mum, but I'm sure she'll say yes. I can't believe I might get to meet Rachel Mint!'

'You can call your mom from Daddy's cell phone!' Leslie yelled as she ran down the hall back to class. 'Meet me after school by the back door. That's where he's picking us up!'

'Perfect!' Nicole thought. 'That way I can avoid having to tell the English Roses.'

She was so excited she could hardly stand still. Even though it seemed babyish, she couldn't resist skipping back to class (she prayed no cute boys would see her). A dark cloud passed through her mind as she thought of the Roses – they were *really* counting on her – but she pushed it away. This was an event that was *really* T.G.T.B.T. – too good to be true!

CHAPTER 5

Forget the Dance?!

Awesome!

Awesome!

Awesome!

'You should have been there, Mum,' Nicole exclaimed as she happily munched her cereal with soya milk. 'It was sooo awesome. The most awesome of the awesomely awesome things that have ever happened to me! I shook her hand! Then

Leslie's dad took a picture of us with her – with Rachel Mint! AND I got to touch her guitar. Rachel Mint's guitar! She's the best singer I've ever heard!'

'Sounds like you had a good time last night.' Mrs Rissman smiled, pouring Nicole a glass of orange juice. 'But were you supposed to do something with the English Roses? They called here last night looking for you.'

At the mention of the Roses, Nicole had a funny feeling in the pit of her stomach. 'Well,' she stammered, 'I did say I would practise our talent-show dance with them after school. But then Leslie told me about this Rachel Mint thing, and I really wanted to go, and I guess I figured they would understand.'

Talking talent-show tactics!

'Don't you think it was rude of you not to let them know, though?' Mrs Rissman said slowly. 'They're your best friends!'

Nicole's face burned with shame. She knew what she had done was wrong, but secretly, she was almost glad she had missed boring dance practice.

Suddenly there was a loud honking in the driveway.

'Gotta go, Mum,' Nicole said, draining her glass of orange juice and flying out the door. 'Leslie's dad is driving us to school today,' she called as the door slammed after her.

* * *

In the car, Leslie threw her arms round Nicole and shrieked, 'Wasn't last night the bestest time EVER?'

'Leslie, please, keep the volume down a bit, will you?' said Mr Loehmann from the front seat of the family's Land Rover. 'I'm only on my first cup of coffee.'

'Thanks so much for inviting me last night, Mr Loehmann,' Nicole said softly. 'I really did have a lot of fun.' Nicole always felt shy around Mr Loehmann.

'Glad to hear it!' Mr Loehmann replied, pulling up in front of the school. 'Have fun and behave yourselves, girls.'

After they said goodbye to Mr Loehmann and hopped out of the car, Leslie threw her arm round Nicole. 'Wouldn't it be cool if we could do something together for the talent show?' she said wistfully. 'I can just picture it: you singing your song, me on guitar . . . it would be just like . . . like a double dose of Rachel Mint!'

Nicole bit her lip. The truth was, deep down inside, she would rather do her song with Leslie than the dance with the English Roses. But she didn't want to hurt her friends' feelings. And she had already committed to doing a dance with them.

'That would be double cool, Leslie,' she said. 'But honestly, I just wouldn't feel right about ditching the English Roses.'

'No, I totally understand,' Leslie said. 'I just

thought it would be fun.' She paused. 'Actually, I think your friends hate me.'

'What?!' Nicole asked, shocked. The idea had never even entered her mind. 'Why on earth would you say that?'

'I don't know,' Leslie said, shaking her head, 'it's just a feeling I get. I'm clearly an outsider.'

'That's ridiculous,' said Nicole, waving the notion away with her hand. 'I know for a fact they love you!'

Let me just fill you in on something: That statement wasn't exactly true. The English Roses did *not* love Leslie, though they hadn't told Nicole as much. In fact, Nicole realized that the English Roses really hadn't said anything at all about Leslie since her arrival.

'I guess . . . if you say so.' Leslie shrugged, not sounding entirely sure. 'Well, ta-ta! I gotta get to class.' And she was off, flying down the hall.

Nicole started fiddling with the combination to her locker when she felt someone hovering over her. Then two someones. Then three. Then four. She looked up to find the English Roses glaring at her.

'Hey, guys, what's up?' Nicole said, flashing a weak smile.

'Oh, nothing,' Grace said icily. 'We're just glad to see that you're alive, that's all. When you didn't show up for dance practice we thought . . . oh, I don't know . . . that maybe someone had kidnapped you, or you fell off London Bridge, because a *real* friend would never stand someone up like that.'

'Listen, I'm so sorry, something came up at the last minute, and –'

Amy cut her off. 'I don't get it, Nicole. What could have been so important that you had to ditch us? It's like you're becoming a total –'

'I think what Amy's trying to say,' Binah interrupted, 'is that we were worried about you when you didn't show up last night, because it's so unlike you to do something like that.'

Nicole took a deep breath. She could feel her face flushing. 'I was planning to come to practice, but Leslie's father got us backstage passes to see Rachel Mint, and we had to leave right after school, so there wasn't time to tell you. I'm really sorry. I'll be there tonight, okay?'

'Oh, I should have known it was *Leslie*,' Amy said disgustedly.

'Why are we even bothering to do this dance?' Grace asked angrily. 'It's obvious you aren't fully committed. Even Charlotte, who's not the world's best dancer – sorry, Char, but it's true – shows up to practice every day. But you're far too busy with lame-o Leslie –'

'Hey, that's not fair,' Nicole interrupted her. 'Don't start blaming Leslie.'

'We're not blaming her,' Charlotte said. 'It's just that ever since Leslie moved here, we hardly see you any more. It's like she's trying to steal you away from us.'

'That's ridiculous!' snapped Nicole. 'You're totally making that up!'

'Well, maybe the truth is, we don't like Leslie. She's stuck up and mean and thinks she's so cool, but she's not!' Amy snapped. The other girls nodded their heads in agreement.

Nicole felt anger rising within her like steam. So this is how the English Roses welcomed her friend!

She couldn't believe she felt so guilty ditching them last night. If this was the kind of people they were, she didn't want to be a part of their dance!

'Just forget the dance, okay? I don't want to do it anyway. I don't know why you girls are being so mean and gossipy, but I don't really want to be around you right now. Now, if you'll excuse me, I have to get to class.'

She slammed her locker and whirled round, stomping off. Binah ran after her. 'Nicole, wait!' The first bell rang.

Charlotte grabbed Binah's arm. 'Just forget it, Binah,' she said. 'We don't need her anyway.' And with that, the four remaining English Roses linked arms and tramped angrily down the hall.

CHAPTER 6

Sometimes Friends Do Silly Things

At break, instead of sitting with the English Roses on the bench in front of the football field, gossiping about cute players and the day's events, Nicole rushed to find Leslie. She was standing in the middle of a gaggle of girls, who were hanging on to her every word.

'And then I was all – no I'm *not* going to your dumb party, because I think you're lame, and do you KNOW who my father is?'

'Hey, Leslie,' Nicole interrupted. 'Can I talk to you for a sec?'

I know, I know, right now, you're probably thinking: this Leslie girl seems pretty obnoxious, so why did Nicole like her in the first place?

Well, she didn't act like that *all* the time. In fact, most of the time Leslie was actually a delightful young lady. But you have to remember that she was the new kid in school, and she desperately wanted people to like her, so she sometimes acted like a bit of a show-off. Haven't *you* ever showed off a tiny bit to impress someone? Anyway, back to our story.

The two girls moved slightly apart from the rest of the group.

'I was thinking . . . are you still up for doing a song for the talent show?' Nicole asked. 'Because that dance thing . . . it's kind of not happening any more.'

Leslie's face broke into a huge grin. 'OF COURSE!' she shrieked. 'How awesome will that be? We'll win first prize, for sure.' She threw her arms around Nicole and the two jumped up and down excitedly.

They spent the rest of break planning their

number. Leslie would strum the guitar while Nicole belted out the song. They discussed important matters such as lighting and costumes (Leslie's father might be able to get something from the movie studio's wardrobe department).

When the bell rang, Leslie disappeared into

Mr Farburger's classroom, while Nicole sauntered into Mrs Moss's. Head held high, she slipped into her seat next to Amy, careful not to look at her or any of the other Roses.

'My my, we certainly are wound up today!' Mrs Moss said with a smile as she stood before her class. 'Please pipe down, everybody.

I have an important announcement to make!'

A hush fell over the room. Usually a teacher telling them to be quiet didn't do much, but for some reason, when Mrs Moss wanted silence, her students felt compelled to give it to her.

'Just a quick reminder,' she said brightly, 'that the talent show is next Tuesday after school in the gymnasium. Don't forget that we have some fabulous prizes up for grabs – for example, a gift certificate for Harrods, and a day out in London with year-seven teacher Miss Fluffernutter – and she's known as a pretty fun lady around these parts.'

The class giggled.

'Now, please get out your books,' she continued. 'Today we'll continue our discussion of Elizabeth George Speare's *The Witch of Blackbird Pond.*

Would any of you care to summarize the story thus far?'

Jenny Brixton raised her hand. 'Well, it takes place in the 1600s. Kit, the main character, lives in Barbados, but after her parents die she is forced to move in with her aunt in a Puritan colony in Weathersfield, Connecticut. None of the Puritans, including her aunt, are nice to her. They don't approve of her and they think she may be a witch.'

'Very good, Jenny. And why aren't the Puritans friendly to Kit?' Mrs Moss asked.

Nicole raised her hand. 'I think it's simply because everyone in Weathersfield is prejudiced against Kit. She's new and from a different place and they feel threatened and jealous of her. It's very unfair of them.'

Amy raised her hand next. 'I agree that it's sad,' she said. 'But I wonder if it wouldn't be better if Kit made more of an effort to fit in.'

'I also wonder how Kit treated people back home,' Grace chimed in. 'She doesn't seem the type of girl who would ever betray her best friends. That's part of what makes me like her so much.'

'Thank you, Grace,' Mrs Moss said, a smile playing on her lips. 'But in this class we raise our hands when we want to speak. That way we can make sure that everyone hears what others have to say.'

Nicole looked over at Grace, who glared back at her. She sighed and bit her nails. This was going to be hard. She had never got into a real fight with the English Roses before. Sure, they'd had arguments over silly things, like who was the coolest dancer, or whose house was best for sleepovers, but they'd always made up right away. When the bell rang, she gathered up her books and bolted out of the classroom. She needed to get home and think.

*   *   *

Nicole's mum was at home making spicy salsa in the blender. There was already a bowl of it on the table next to an open bag of tortilla chips – Nicole's favourite. Mrs Rissman's usual cheerful expression changed to one of concern when she saw the glum look on her daughter's face.

'What's wrong, Miss Moody?' she asked, gathering Nicole into a hug and kissing her messy blonde head.

'Bad day,' said Nicole, grabbing a handful of

tortilla chips and piling them with salsa. 'The English Roses are being impossible, Mum. I just – YOWWWWWW!'

'Oops – honey, I meant to throw that batch out. I accidentally put too many chilli peppers in it,' Mrs Rissman said, handing Nicole a glass of water. 'Drink this. It will make you feel better. So – they *were* angry at you for ditching practice last night?'

'Well, it started out that way,' Nicole began, chugging the water, 'but then they started saying mean things about Leslie. I just can't believe they'd treat a new girl that way. Especially a girl who's my friend!'

Nicole's mother thought a minute. 'Maybe, honey,' she suggested, 'they're just envious that you're spending so much time with Leslie. Maybe they just miss their friend.'

'Friend? Yeah, some friends they are. Why wouldn't they just say something,' fumed Nicole, 'instead of acting like such silly, selfish brats!'

'Sometimes friends do silly things,' her mum reminded her. 'Remember last year, when you and the others ignored Binah all the time before you got to know her? Maybe you should try to talk to them.'

Nicole shook her head furiously. 'No way. I don't want to be friends with girls who act that way. I'm out of the talent-show dance. In fact, I'm performing my song instead . . . with Leslie on guitar!'

Mrs Rissman beamed. '*The* song? The one you've been working on for so long? Nicole, honey,

I'm so proud of you!'

'Well, I have to finish it first, Mum,' Nicole said.

'I still think you should talk to the English Roses, though,' Mrs Rissman added.

Nicole rolled her eyes. She stuffed a few more chips in her mouth and ran upstairs to her room.

*　*　*

Sprawled on her bed, notebook and pen in hand, Nicole lazily played with her hair. She was stuck on the song's chorus; it was the most important part, and yet she couldn't figure out exactly what she wanted to say. Originally the song was about best friends; she felt inspired to write it after the big autumn dance last year, at which the English Roses

had made amends after a pretty big brawl. All of the girls had had the biggest crush on Dominic de la Guardia, the handsome, funny, smart and kind foreign exchange student, but he had paid attention only to Binah. Consequently, the girls had treated

Binah badly, but Miss Fluffernutter convinced them that their friendship was way more important than a cute boy. Dominic had ended up moving back to Spain at the end of year seven, though Binah and he still kept in touch.

Now the thought of her former best friends didn't inspire any creativity, only anger. She felt almost as if they had changed personalities overnight. It was sad to remember all of the good times they had had together ... and for what?

To take her mind off the Roses, Nicole logged on to her computer. She checked her IM buddies list— Amy was online, but she'd rather bathe in a pile of upchuck than talk to her. Triple ick! She looked at the wall above her computer, which was plastered with snapshots of her and the Roses at sleepovers, ice skating in the park, fancy-dress parties. . . .

She flopped back on the bed dramatically and heaved a giant sigh. Forgetting the English Roses was going to be a lot more difficult than she'd hoped.

CHAPTER 7

A Case of Writer's Block

'No no no, you were wayyyy too high on that note,' sighed Leslie. 'Remember, *soulful*, Nikki. Let's try it again, from the top, please.'

Nicole rolled her eyes. It was the second afternoon of practice with Leslie, and so far, her friend was turning out to be a drill sergeant. She claimed to have a specific 'vision' of the 'piece' (that's what she called it: a 'piece,' like she was the conductor of a symphony or something!), and would stop at nothing until it was performed perfectly. Nicole was more than a little irked.

'It is my song, you know,' Nicole muttered under her breath.

'What was that?' Leslie asked, manically tuning her guitar. 'Argh! I broke a string!'

Nicole winced. 'I need a drink of water or something; my throat's parched.'

'Okay, we'll take five, but no more than that,' Leslie conceded. 'The contest is the day after tomorrow, remember!'

'Oh, I remember,' Nicole said. She stood up and stretched her legs, chugging from a water bottle.

Leslie fiddled with her guitar, flipping ahead in

the music sheets Nicole had given her. Suddenly,
she shrieked.

Alarmed, Nicole shrieked too. 'What is it???!!!
OH MY GOD, IS IT A SPIDER? I HATE
spiders more than ANYTHING. Kill it! Kill IT.
EWWWWW!'

Oh, and I should mention one more thing about the English Roses: their habit of constantly shrieking is really out of control. It's enough to drive one mad!

Leslie looked at her as if she were an alien from another planet. 'No, not a spider. Nikki, you didn't finish writing the chorus.'

Nicole looked down at her feet. It was true, she hadn't been able to finish the chorus. She had tried and tried, but nothing had come to her. She was stuck.

'I sorta have a case of writer's block,' she said, chewing on her fingernail. 'Everything was going really well, and then for some reason, when I got to the chorus, it just dried up.'

Leslie's voice became strained. 'Well, we can't do

the talent show without a chorus. I'll have to dream
something up if the inspiration gods don't shine on
you by Tuesday.'

'Look, I'll try to write something tonight!' Nicole
said, throwing up her hands in exasperation. 'You
don't need to go for a medal in the Pushy Olympics.
Can we please just continue practising?'

'Oh, Nikki, I'm sorry!' Leslie said. 'I just want
everything to be perfect. I don't mean to act like a
brat.'

'That's okay,' Nicole replied sheepishly. 'I guess
I'm just super-nervous about finishing the song in
time.'

'Well, I've got something that will take your
mind off the song,' Leslie gushed excitedly. 'Wait
right here!'

She left the room, only to return with two sparkly outfits on hangers. 'What do you think of these? My dad says they should fit us!'

Nicole gasped as she fingered the clothes. 'These are T.D.F. – to die for!' she squealed, astonished. 'Where did your dad find them?'

'Oh, a friend of a friend,' Leslie grinned. 'Some singer almost wore them, apparently, on her last tour. Aren't they fabulous? We'll definitely be the stars of the show in these.'

Nicole fingered the delicate embellishment on the bodice of one of the costumes. 'Amy would go crazy for this,' she thought. She felt a twinge of sadness as she remembered that she couldn't tell Amy about the costumes. Amy was no longer her friend.

The truth was, she missed the English Roses.

Dancing, guitars and shining stars!

She missed their break-time giggling sessions and their five-way phone calls after school each night. She even missed dance practice! Suddenly Nicole realized just how much the English Roses really meant to her. She knew she had been wrong to ditch them for the Rachel Mint concert – at the very least she could have called them to let them know she wasn't showing up for practice that afternoon. It fully dawned on Nicole that she had hurt her friends terribly. But what could she do to win them back? Especially with the talent show just two days away!

An idea popped in her head. 'I've gotta go home,' she told Leslie, jumping up and dusting off her jeans. 'I just remembered something I have to do.'

CHAPTER 8

Best Friends Always, Jill the End

inner's ready, sweetie,' Mrs Rissman said as she poked her head in Nicole's room.

'Um . . . I'm kinda right in the middle of something, Mum. Is there any way I can eat dinner later? Please?'

Nicole's mother gave her a stern look. Family dinners were very important in the Rissman family, especially since Mr Rissman wasn't home that much. But she could see that her daughter was working intensely. 'Well, I suppose this once, since you seem to be in the Zone. What are you working on, anyway?'

'The Zone' was the term Mrs Rissman gave to Nicole's intensity when she worked on any creative project. It meant she was in another world.

'For the first time in ages, I think I've got my creative juices back, Mum,' she said, smiling. 'And hopefully tomorrow I'll have the English Roses back too.'

Messy hair flying as her pen flew across the page, Nicole finished what she was writing with a flourish. It was perfect! It was heartfelt! It couldn't be any better. But the best thing was, it totally rocked!

Now she just had two phone calls to make. Two *very important* phone calls.

First she rang Leslie. She told her that she had finished the song, and could she come over after dinner so they could practise it together? Leslie agreed.

The second call was going to be a bit more difficult. Nicole picked up the phone, took a deep breath, and dialled Binah's number. If she was going to do this, better start with the most gentle of all the Roses.

Binah's soft voice answered on the second ring. 'Hello, Rossi residence.'

'Binah, hey, it's Nicole.'

'Oh, hi, Nicole,' Binah said brightly. Nicole couldn't tell if she was really happy to hear from

her or just being polite. 'I was just finishing up the dinner dishes,' she added.

'Listen, I feel really bad about what's happened between us, all of us, the English Roses and Leslie and . . . me. I want to be friends again. But I can't do it without your help.'

'Okay,' Binah said hesitantly. 'What do you want me to do?'

'Just get all of the Roses to meet in the gym during break tomorrow,' Nicole told her. 'Don't tell them what it is. Say it's a surprise.'

'Uhhh . . . they're going to be suspicious. And it's the day before the talent show, so Grace is probably going to want to use break to practise.'

'Tell Grace this is about the talent show,' Nicole said. 'You won't be sorry. This is big.'

She said goodbye, hung up the phone and broke into an excited, breathless prance all around her room. If all went smoothly, the English Roses would be her friends again in no time.

* * *

The next day, heads held high, Amy, Charlotte, Grace and Binah strutted into the dark gymnasium.

'What the heck is going on here?' Grace demanded.

'Binah, is this some sort of prank?' Amy complained, tossing her flaming-red hair in annoyance. 'Because it's *sooo* not funny.'

Suddenly, a spotlight shone on Leslie and Nicole, who were both perched on stools in the middle

of the gym. They were decked out in the most ultra-glam outfits the English Roses had ever seen. Both were wearing fitted minidresses sequinned all over in a sparkly silver pattern. Nicole had a microphone in her hand. Her blonde hair was not pulled back in its usual messy ponytail, but hung down her shoulders in a straight golden waterfall. Leslie stood next to her with a pink electric guitar splattered with silver stars. The guitar had a sparkly silver strap that was wrapped around her shoulder. Both girls' nails were painted a deep red with tiny silver stars pasted on the middle.

Annoyed as she was, Amy couldn't conceal a little gasp at the sheer magnificence of their outfits. They looked like stylin' rock stars.

The gym reverberated with Nicole's heavenly

vocals while Leslie plucked away at the guitar. The girls' jaws dropped. Nicole's voice was so deep and pure, so clear and smooth and strong – they could hardly believe it was coming from the same moody, quiet Nicole Rissman they knew so well. But even more beautiful were the words to the song:

> 'Just as long as we're together
> We've got loads of sunny weather.
> Best friends always, till the end,
> The sun won't shine without my friends.'

It was a rockin' song, and Leslie was quite a talented guitar player. As she played, the Roses could feel their anger slowly melting away. When they were finished, the English Roses couldn't help but give them a standing ovation.

'I'm so happy you came,' Nicole said as she hopped off her stool. 'I've been dying to talk to you. I miss you all so much!'

'Yeah, us too,' said Grace. 'It stinks not being friends with you, Nicole.' The other girls nodded in agreement.

'No, I stink for being such a brat,' Nicole said. 'I'm super-sorry for ditching you for that concert. It was a nasty thing to do. The best friends ever don't deserve to be treated like that.'

'And we're sorry for getting so mad about Leslie,' said Grace. She turned to Leslie. 'I feel really bad about not making more of an effort to be friendly to you.'

Leslie smiled. 'Well, I've been acting kind of snobalicious, too. I hope you know I don't mean it.

I was just so nervous to meet the English Roses. All I had heard about was how wonderful you were, and I wanted to make sure you all liked me. Guess I didn't exactly come off as the coolest American girl ever.'

'Still friends for life?' Nicole asked.

'Friends for life!' the other girls cried.

'But what about the talent show?' Grace said. 'Our dance routine just doesn't have the same oomph with only four of us. Not to mention, with your bangin' song and look, we don't have a chance at winning!'

'I have a crazy idea,' said Leslie. 'Why don't we all perform together? I hear that you girls –' she motioned to the English Roses – 'are marvellous dancers. Why don't you dance to Nicole's song, and

I'll play the guitar? Six times the coolness!'

'But what about the name?' asked Charlotte.

'That's easy,' smiled Grace. 'We can be the Sassy Six – *soo* much better than the Funky Five!'

'Brilliant, Grace!' Binah smiled.

'Oh, yeah,' Leslie said. 'Or as you say over here, totally brill!'

The other girls giggled. The six of them linked arms and walked to class just as the bell rang.

CHAPTER 9

Night of the Stars

Yeah, my rhymes be tight; this you ought-ta know. If my nose starts to drip I just cut the flow; Word up, word up, word up, y'all.'

The Sassy Six stifled giggles back-stage at the talent show as they watched Harold Fieldbinder frantically attempt his hip-hop routine.

Poor Harold, the skinniest kid in school, also suffered from an acute case of postnasal drip. To top it off, he fancied himself London's hottest MC. For the occasion of the talent show, his skinny frame was encased in a white tank top with about a million gold medallions layered over it. He was also wearing a baseball cap backwards and sunglasses that were half the size of his pimply face.

'Please give a big round of applause for Mr Fieldbinder, as MC Drip-Drop,' Miss Fluffernutter, acting as the show's MC, said while ushering Harold offstage. He continued yelling 'Yeah, y'all!' all the way back to the dressing room.

'Thank you. Our next act is sure to be a crowd-pleaser! Please give a warm welcome to the Sassy Six in a special song/dance routine, with Nicole

Rissman on vocals and our visiting student, Leslie Loehmann, on guitar.'

Polite clapping ensued as the curtain rose to reveal Nicole and Leslie, sparkly as stars, perched on their stools. Behind them stood Charlotte, Grace, Amy and Binah, dressed to the nines in glittering silver outfits, their arms and necks laden with fancy costume jewellery, courtesy of Amy's mum, who worked for a department store and was able to get hold of merchandise months before the general public.

The gymnasium rang with Nicole's sweet alto as Leslie forcefully strummed her guitar. Techno beats boomed behind them as the rest of the girls swayed rhythmically. Grace bounded across the stage in an impressive series of flips, while Amy and Charlotte held Binah up in a mini-version of a pyramid. As the song finished with a flourish, glittery confetti rained down on the girls from above.

The applause was deafening. The entire gymnasium was on its collective feet clapping and stomping for the English Roses. The girls could hardly contain their excitement. Nicole and Leslie beamed at each other, then at the rest of the Roses, and finally at the crowd.

'Those girls have really outdone themselves!' Charlotte heard someone in the audience remark.

'They're soooo awesome,' another person said. 'This was by far the best thing I've seen all night.'

The girls jumped and skipped offstage. When it was finally time for Miss Fluffernutter to name the winner, they could hardly keep still.

'Second prize goes to Bunny Love and Candy Darling for their fantabulous tap dance! Bunny and Candy, please claim your gift certificate for Yummy House of Flapjacks.'

Bunny and Candy click-clacked onstage in their tap shoes and waved happily to the audience as they accepted an envelope from Miss Fluffernutter.

'And now, the moment we've all been waiting for – or at least, I know I have,' Miss Fluffernutter chuckled, kicking up her heels with glee. 'This year's grand prize winner is . . . the Sassy Six!'

The girls squealed as they hugged each other in astonished glee. They bounded onstage, jumping up and down as Miss Fluffernutter squeezed each one of them.

Nicole asked Miss Fluffernutter if she could say a few words, and Miss Fluffernutter handed her the microphone. 'Please, no hip-hop speak,' she whispered to Nicole with a smile.

'I just wanted to say,' Nicole began timidly, 'that I want to thank these five girls for being the best friends ever. I didn't realize how much I appreciated them until we weren't friends any more. And just so you know, when it comes to friendship, the old cliché is true: you don't know what you've got till it's gone! So everyone out there, be sure to appreciate your friends. They're the most important thing you've got!'

The audience clapped as the girls hugged each other again.

'I can't believe what awesome dancers you girls are!' Leslie gushed. 'My friends at home aren't nearly as good!'

'Aww, thanks, Leslie.' Grace smiled.

'In fact,' Leslie continued, a gleam in her eye, 'I think I should have a party to celebrate the fabulous friends I've made in London. Who wants to come over to my house on Saturday for the biggest chocolate sundae-making extravanganza ever?!'

'Sounds awesome!' Amy said. 'Leslie, what are we going to do when you go back to New York?'

As soon as she said it, Amy and the other girls realized how much they'd really miss Leslie when she left. She had turned out to be quite an English Rose on the inside. Didn't I tell you that you can't judge someone until you really get to know them . . . even if they seem to be snobby at first?

'I don't know,' Leslie said sadly. 'I'm going to really miss you all.'

'That's why we have to make the most of the time we have together!' Binah announced as she put her arm around Leslie.

'Yeah,' Charlotte agreed. 'Like, have as many sundae-making parties as possible!'

'The English Roses would never miss a party – especially one with ice cream,' Grace giggled. ''Cause we do eat a lot of that over here, right?'

'Are you kidding? It's got to be my favourite thing about the Brits!' Leslie smiled. The six girls linked arms as they walked down the hall.

The End

MADONNA RITCHIE was born in Bay City, Michigan, and now lives in London and Los Angeles with her husband, movie director Guy Ritchie, and her children, Lola, Rocco and David. She has recorded 17 albums and appeared in 18 movies. This is the third in her series of chapter books. She has also written six picture books for children, starting with the international bestseller *The English Roses*, which was released in 40 languages and more than 100 countries.

PICTURE BOOKS:

Mr Peabody's Apples
Yakov and the Seven Thieves
The Adventures of Abdi
Lotsa de Casha
The English Roses: Too Good To Be True

CHAPTER BOOKS:

Friends for Life!
Goodbye, Grace?
A Rose by Any Other Name

JEFFREY FULVIMARI was born in Akron, Ohio. He started colouring when he was two, and has never stopped. Soon after graduating from The Cooper Union in New York, he began drawing for magazines and television commercials around the globe. He currently lives in a log cabin in upstate New York, and is happiest when surrounded by stacks of paper and magic markers.